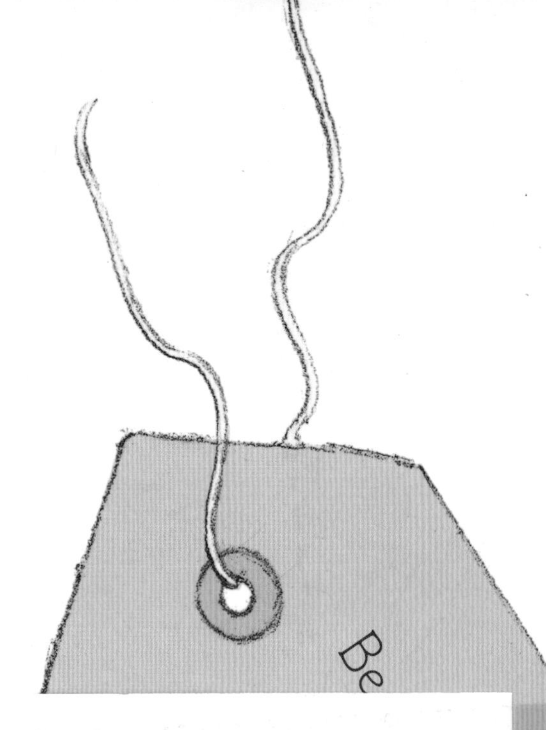

Aberdeenshire Library and Information Service
www.aberdeenshire.gov.uk/libraries

ORCHARD BOOKS
338 Euston Road, London NW1 3BH
Orchard Books Australia
Level 17/207 Kent Street, Sydney, NSW 2000

First published in 2008 by Orchard Books
First published in paperback in 2009

A CIP catalogue record for this book
is available from the British Library.

ISBN 978 1 84616 307 4

1 3 5 7 9 10 8 6 4 2

Printed in China
Orchard Books is a division of Hachette Children's Books,
an Hachette UK Company.
www.hachette.co.uk

The Bear with Sticky Paws Goes to School

Clara Vulliamy

ORCHARD BOOKS

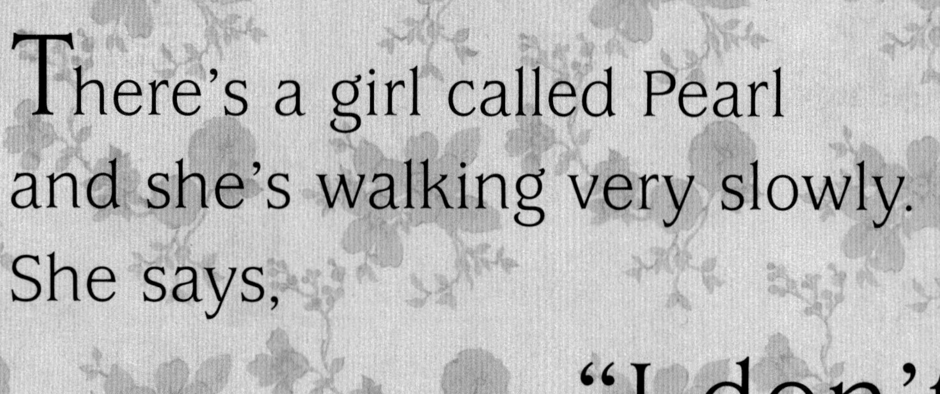

There's a girl called Pearl
and she's walking very slowly.
She says,

"I don't
want to go to
school today!"

"Hurry up, Pearl," says Mum.
"We'll be late!"

"But it's just too silly at school.

I've got no one to play with.

I want to stay at home!"

And –

CRASH!

– down goes
her bag!

But then,
bing-
bong!

There's a bear on the doorstep,
a small white tufty one,
standing on his suitcase to reach the bell.

"Come to my school!"
says the bear.

"It's FUN at Bear School!"

"Do we hang our coats up here?"
asks Pearl.

"NO!" says the bear.
"We throw them in the air!"

"OK," says Pearl.

"Sit down, everyone!" says the bear.
"Are we all here? Pearl?"

"Yes!" says Pearl.

"ME? Oh YES!" says the bear.
"Now, let's get started ..."

"What will we do first?" asks Pearl.

"PAINTING!"

says the bear.

Pearl paints

1 red house, 2 orange cats
and 3 yellow ducks.

The bear paints

1 BIG BLUE BEAR.

And – oh NO!

Sticky paws everywhere!

"MUSIC TIME!" says the bear.

"Oh good!" says Pearl.

The bear plays ALL the instruments –

1 pink piano,

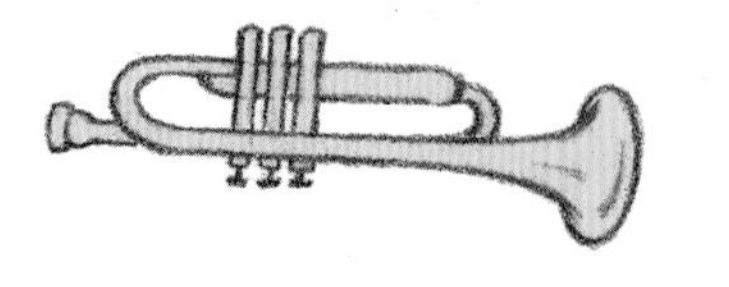

2 tooting trumpets,

3 crashing cymbals . . .

and 1 great big drum . . .

And –

oh NO!

Too noisy!

"Time for COOKING!"

says the bear.

Pearl makes

1 gingerbread man,

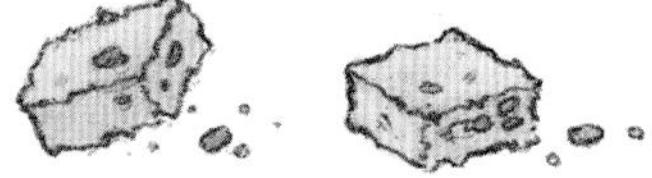

2 fruity flapjacks

and 3 fairy cakes.

The bear makes
1 BIG GOOEY MESS.

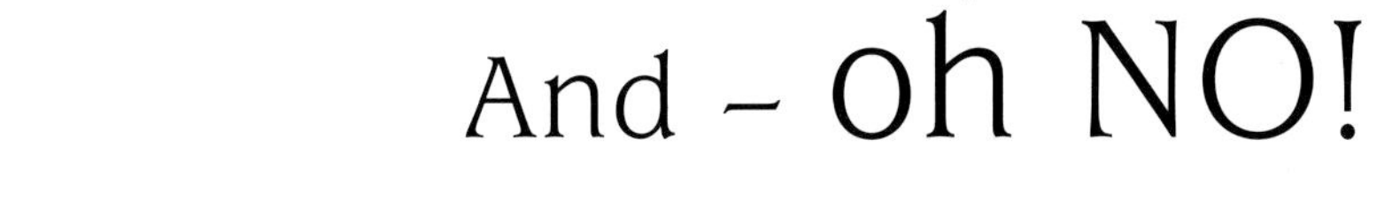

And – oh NO!
Sticky paws everywhere!

"Is it story time?" asks Pearl.

"YES!" says the bear.

"WORRA
WORRA
WORRA
WORRA . . ."

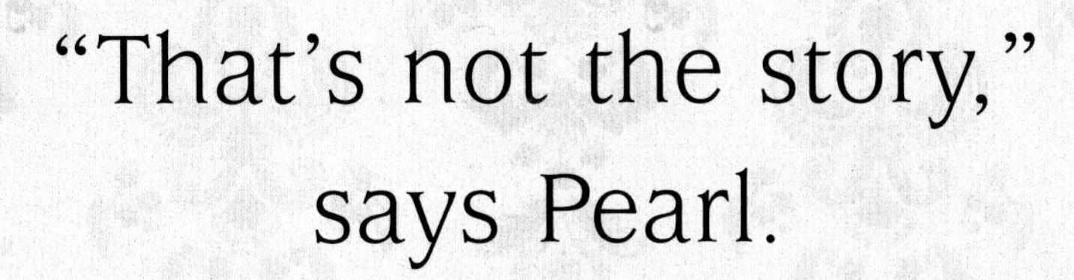

"That's not the story,"
says Pearl.

"No more story!"
says the bear.

"It's jelly time!"

"It's nice to share," says Pearl.

"Not share!"
says the bear.
"ALL FOR ME!"

"I want to do my numbers," says Pearl.

"*I* want to do CARS!"

says the bear.

And – oh NO!
Everything gets knocked over!

"Let's play shop!" says Pearl.
"What would you like to buy?"

"EVERYTHING!"
says the bear.

And – oh NO!

He runs off with the trolley.

"Wait for me!" says Pearl.

"OUTSIDE!"

says the bear.

And — oh NO!

CRASH!

Down comes everything!

"That's *enough*," says Pearl.
"I've had enough of Bear School.

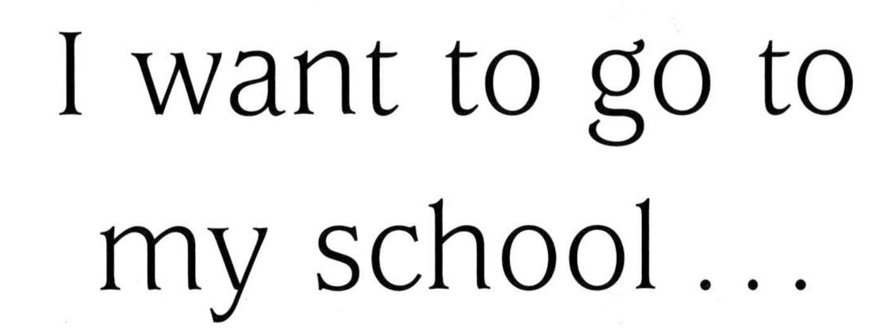

I want to go to
my school . . .

GOODBYE!"

"I'm ready," says Pearl.
"Wait for me, Mum."

"Let's go!" says Mum,
holding her hand.

And Pearl hops,

skips

and jumps

all the way to school,

arriving just in time …

to have a happy wave goodbye …

...and make 1 new friend.

Reward Chart

Name:	Name:			Name:	
On school days . . .	Monday	Tuesday	Wednesday	Thursday	Friday
I will get dressed					
I will brush my teeth					
I will pack my book bag					
I won’t be late					
I will do cutting and sticking					
I will paint a lovely picture					
I will be friendly					
I will listen at story-time					
I will come home happy					
I will					
I will					
I will					

After ____ paw stickers,
I wish for ______________.

After ____ paw stickers,
I wish for ______________.

After ____ paw stickers,
I wish for ______________.